Frankie Is Staying Back

Frankie stared at his sandwich. His bottom lip started to wiggle up and down. His eyes turned shiny. "I'm staying back," he said to his best friend Jonas.

Frankie and Jonas have been close friends ever since they were little, and they're in the same third grade class. Frankie has trouble with reading, but neither he nor Jonas takes the problem seriously until the day Frankie learns he will have to repeat third grade. Jonas will be going on to fourth grade without him, and both boys fear that their separation in school will mean the end of their friendship.

As Jonas tries to think of a way for him and Frankie to remain together, the author shapes a touching story of failure, hope—and true friendship.

Frankie Is Staying Back

FRANKIE IS STAYING BACK

by RON ROY
Pictures by WALTER KESSELL

CLARION BOOKS

TICKNOR & FIELDS : A HOUGHTON MIFFLIN COMPANY
NEW YORK

Clarion Books
Ticknor & Fields, a Houghton Mifflin Company

Text copyright © 1981 by Ron Roy.
Illustrations copyright © 1981 by Walter Kessell.

Printed in the United States of America.

Library of Congress Cataloging in Publication Data
Roy, Ronald, 1940–   Frankie is staying back.
Summary: When his best friend has to repeat third grade, Jonas tries to think of a way for them to remain in the same class.
[1. School stories.   2. Friendship—Fiction]   I. Title.
PZ7.R8139Fe   [Fic]   80-28257
ISBN 0-395-31025-3

*This book is dedicated to
all children who have stayed back,
and to their parents and teachers.*
R.R.

chapter 1

Jonas glanced around the cafeteria and spotted his best friend, Frankie. He forced his way through a bunch of fifth-graders, and slid in beside him on the bench.

"Where's your lunch?" Jonas shouted above the racket as he tore into his own. Frankie didn't answer. He sat slumped like a scarecrow that had slid off its pole.

Jonas shrugged, then pulled a carefully wrapped mound of tinfoil out of his lunch bag. He laid it gently in front of Frankie, as if it were a bomb.

"Mom made it for you," he lied. "It's your favorite—fried egg sandwich."

Frankie stared into space.

"Come on, Frankfurter," Jonas begged. "Open it. Mom made it just for *you.*"

Frankie sighed and sat up a little straighter. He opened the folds of tinfoil as if he had all day to eat lunch instead of twenty-two minutes. It wasn't a fried egg sandwich. It was a rubber snake between two slices of pumpernickel bread.

"APRIL FOOL!" Jonas shouted.

Frankie shoved the snake aside. He looked as if he'd just swallowed a burning match.

Jonas couldn't believe it. He took a bite of his onion, avocado, and cheese sandwich. "What's the matter with you, anyway?" he mumbled around the mouthful.

"You're disgusting," Frankie muttered.

"It talks!" Jonas cried, whamming his friend on the back. "Seriously, want part of my lunch?"

"I'm never eating again," Frankie said. It was almost a whisper.

Jonas stared at Frankie. He looked as if he

might start crying. Then Jonas remembered how Frankie had been mysteriously called out of gym class.

"Did something happen when you left gym?" he asked.

Frankie stared at the snake sandwich. His bottom lip started to wiggle up and down. His eyes turned shiny. "I'm staying back," he said.

At first Jonas thought he'd heard the wrong words. He thought Frankie was April Fooling him. But Jonas had heard right—Frankie wasn't fooling.

Frankie got up and slouched out of the cafeteria like a yelled-at puppy. Jonas crammed the rest of his sandwich into his mouth, tossed his crumpled bag into the trash can, and raced after his friend.

When he got to the play area he saw Frankie sitting on a swing. Not swinging, just sitting.

"Want me to push you?" Jonas asked.

"No."

"Want to run around and crash into girls?"

"No."

"Want to do *anything?*" Jonas couldn't believe this was the same Frankie he'd walked to school with that morning.

"I want to go home," Frankie whispered.

"Can't," Jonas said. "Two more hours after lunch." He kicked a hole in the sawdust under his swing seat.

"Was that why they pulled you out of gym?"

After a few seconds Frankie nodded.

"They were all there," he said, "even Mom." He twisted in the swing and looked at Jonas. "I thought I'd done something wrong."

"You?" Jonas was wide-eyed. "You never do anything wrong."

"Everybody smiled when I came in," Frankie went on. "I knew it was fake. Even the principal was smiling like he does on the first day of school." He slid off the swing and flopped down on the grass.

"Mr. Winter was *smiling?*" Jonas said. "I wish I'd been there to see that!" He gave up his swing and leaned against one of the metal poles. It was cold on his back. "So what happened?"

A ladybug landed on the back of Frankie's hand. He picked a piece of grass and held it in front of the bug.

"Mr. Winter said, 'Sit down, Francis. Miss Minty and your mother and I have something to discuss with you,' " Frankie said.

"FRANCIS!" Jonas cried. "I didn't know your name was Francis!"

"It isn't," Frankie muttered. He stood up slowly. "It's Frank, after my father." The ladybug marched across the back of Frankie's hand.

Jonas leaned over and retied his sneaker. He felt funny whenever Frankie mentioned his dad. Since Mr. Giordano had left home about a year ago, nobody knew where he was. Their moms talked about him on the phone, but they always lowered their voices when Jonas was around.

At first Frankie said his dad was just on a vacation. He'd be back in a week, for sure. But he hadn't come home after a week. Or a month. Pretty soon Frankie stopped talking about his dad and Jonas forgot all about him. But Frankie still waited.

"When they said I was being held back," Frankie continued, "I didn't know what they meant. Until Miss Minty said she might be my teacher again next year." The ladybug stopped at Frankie's shirt cuff. It didn't seem to know whether to go over or under.

Jonas stared at his friend staring at the bug. Minty again next year? With a bunch of little second-graders? Well, they'd be new third-graders really. But still.

The bell rang.

"Mr. Winter said after a few weeks I'd make all new friends," Frankie said. "And I wouldn't even remember I was supposed to be a fourth-grader."

Frankie stopped talking all of a sudden. He sniffed and swiped at his nose with the back of his hand.

"Rats!" he cried, jumping to his feet. "I think I killed the ladybug!"

"No, you didn't." Jonas laughed. "He's sitting on your nose."

Frankie looked cross-eyed down his nose. The

bug stayed still. Frankie took a deep breath and blew. The bug flew into the afternoon.

"What have we got now?" Jonas asked, scrambling to his feet.

"Spelling," Frankie said. "Did you study?"

"A little," Jonas said. "You?"

Frankie shook his head. "Wouldn't matter if I did," he said, brushing the seat of his pants. "I get most of the words wrong anyway. Maybe I *should* be a third-grader again."

The final after-lunch bell clanged again. Jonas followed Frankie as they were swallowed up by about a hundred kids trying to get through the door at the same time. His sandwich had turned into a softball in his stomach.

What was he going to do about Frankie?

chapter 2

Jonas and Frankie walked home together after school. Jonas was filled with ideas.

"Let's stop at the library and tease Mrs. Fitch," he suggested.

"No, thanks," Frankie mumbled.

Jonas was disappointed. Mrs. Fitch was one of their favorite targets. They'd stroll into the children's room at the town library, looking as innocent as butterflies. They'd pull a couple of books off the shelf and pretend to read while they waited for Miss Henny to turn her back. Then they'd tear around the corner into the adult section where Mrs. Fitch sat.

There they did their mischief. Like turning all the encyclopedias upside down. Or making animal noises. Once they started singing "Old Mac-Donald Had a Farm." But they got caught in the middle of "eeyi, eeyi, ooohh."

Jonas tried again.

"Want to go to the pet shop and teach the parrots to swear?"

Frankie hesitated. Jonas thought he had him. Frankie loved the pet shop.

"I guess not," Frankie said finally. "I don't really feel like doing anything. I think I'll go home and take a nap."

Take a *nap!* Frankie must be really upset, Jonas thought. Frankie hated naps. Back when their moms used to stick them in the same baby carriage, Frankie's mom always complained that Frankie would never stay put for his nap. In his crib, Frankie would rattle the bars till she lifted him out.

Jonas gave up, disgusted. Here he was, trying to cheer him up, and Frankie was acting like he'd lost his best friend.

"So why are you staying back, anyway?" Jonas

10

asked. He hadn't meant his question to sound so snotty, but it did.

Frankie blushed. "Miss Minty said I'm not ready for fourth grade," he mumbled, staring at the sidewalk. "She said my math and reading are almost the worst in the class."

Jonas slid his eyes around and peeked at Frankie. He looked as if he felt rotten. Jonas didn't feel so hot either. Why did I open my big mouth? he asked himself.

Jonas knew about Frankie's reading. He'd heard him in his reading group for three years. At first nobody seemed to notice that Frankie was having trouble. Then last year everybody practically went crazy when he got really low marks on his reading tests. They put him in Miss Minty's class because she was supposed to be a genius when it came to helping kids with reading problems. It hadn't worked with Frankie.

Jonas didn't know that Frankie was having trouble with math too. But thinking back, he remembered that Frankie *had* asked him for help a couple of times. Had he helped him? Jonas couldn't remember.

"There's still two months till school's out," Jonas said. "Couldn't your mom get a tutor or something?"

Frankie shook his head. "Mom asked at the meeting, but they told her it would be better if I did the whole year over again."

Better for whom, Jonas wondered? They were standing in front of Frankie's house now. Jonas noticed that the grass needed cutting. A few scraggly daffodils waved their yellow heads in the middle of the yard, and weeds were showing around the edges.

"Want to sleep over tonight?" Jonas suggested.

"I don't know," Frankie said. There was a pause. "I'll ask Mom when she gets home from work. It'll probably be late because she had to take some time off to come to school."

"I'll call you later," Jonas promised. " 'Bye."

"See you," Frankie said. He walked up the front sidewalk, fishing his key out of his jeans. Without turning to wave, he let himself into the empty house.

Jonas watched his friend disappear through

the door. He felt depressed. He wanted to make Frankie feel better. But how? He'd have to think about it. Later.

Turning, he ran the two blocks to his own house.

chapter 3

J onas, eat your broccoli, please."

"I hate broccoli."

"You need your greens," his mother insisted. "And besides, you ate three helpings at Nanna's last week."

"She cooks it different," Jonas said, poking at his supper. "With crumbly stuff on top."

"Bread crumbs, dummy," his brother, Dan, put in. "And get your elbows off the table."

"Mind your own business, know-it-all," Jonas snapped.

"Could we please have our dinner without a replay of World War Two?" their father asked.

"What's for dessert?" Beth asked.

"Crickets," Jonas told his little sister. "With bat blood on top."

"MOMMY!" Beth shrieked.

"That's enough, all of you!" Jonas's dad said, smacking the table for emphasis. "What happened to this family today? At breakfast you were humans. Now I'm having dinner with three monsters and I don't like it. Jonas, you apologize, please."

"To who?" Jonas asked.

"To Beth for one," his dad said. "And then to your mother for insulting her broccoli."

"And me," Dan added, "for snooping in my room."

"That's another matter that can be settled by you guys later," their father said. "Jonas?"

"Sorry, Beth," Jonas muttered. "We're not having bat blood and crickets for dessert. The broccoli's okay, Mom. I'm just not hungry, I guess."

"Anything wrong at school?" his father asked.

16

Jonas drew a dinosaur on the tablecloth with the tip of his spoon. "Frankie is staying back," he said finally.

"What?" his mother gasped. "When did this happen? I spoke to Joanne yesterday and she didn't say anything about it."

"He got called to the office during gym," Jonas said. "They told him he wasn't ready for fourth grade. Miss Minty said his math and reading are lousy."

"Somehow I doubt if your teacher used the word 'lousy,' " Jonas's dad said.

"He doesn't act dumb," Dan put in.

"Nobody said Frankie was dumb," his father said, giving Dan a hard look. "How is Frankie taking the bad news, Jonas?"

"Pretty awful, Dad. He moped around all day and wouldn't play after school at all."

He looked at his mother. "Couldn't you do something, Mom?"

"Why, I don't know, Jonas," she said, laying her fork on the edge of her plate. "It's not really my business, is it?"

"But couldn't you talk to the principal, or Miss Minty? Maybe they'd give Frankie another chance."

"That's probably what the school is trying to do, Jonas," his mother replied. "Give him another chance to learn what he missed the first time. But I promise I'll think about it. Now finish your dinner."

Jonas shoveled a pile of mashed potatoes into his mouth and washed it down with milk.

"Poor Joanne," his mother sighed. "First Frank leaves and she has to go to work in that restaurant. Now her kid is staying back. I'd better call her right after supper."

"I asked Frankie to sleep over, okay Mom?" Jonas asked.

"Of course. I'll save him some dessert."

"What's for dessert?" Beth asked once more.

"In a minute, Beth," her mother said. "What time is Frankie coming, Jonas?"

"I don't know. He's supposed to call after his mom gets home from work."

"Well, we'll have our dessert now," Jonas's mother said. "But I'll make sure there's enough left for Frankie."

"WHAT'S FOR DESSERT?" Beth pleaded.

Everyone laughed.

"For you, my sweet little girl," her mother said, glancing around the table with a sly look, "the last of the chocolate ice cream. These boys will have to have something else."

"What?" Jonas and Dan asked together.

"Crickets," their mother said, leaving the dining room.

chapter 4

Frankie showed up at Jonas's house with his pajamas and toothbrush. Everyone acted happy to see him.

"Hiya, Frankie," Jonas's dad said, turning from the program he was watching on television. "How's that pitching arm?"

"Fine, thanks, Mr. Freeman."

"We've saved some dessert for you," Jonas's mother said. "Would you like it now or before you go to bed?"

"I've already had dessert, thanks," Frankie said.

"Well, maybe you and Jonas can have a few cookies later, all right?"

"That'll be fine, thank you," Frankie said.

Nobody mentioned what had happened in school that day, but Jonas guessed that Frankie knew they knew. There was too much smiling going on.

"Jonas, why don't you take Frankie into your room and get him settled," his mother suggested at last.

As soon as the bedroom door closed Frankie whirled around to face Jonas. "Why'd you have to tell?" he demanded hotly.

Jonas felt his face turn red. "I . . . I don't know, it just came out," he stammered. "At supper, we were all talking about school and stuff, and it . . . just came out."

Frankie dropped his pajamas on the bottom bunk. "My mom will call anyway," he said, smiling just a little.

"Yeah," Jonas added, "with the eight o'clock

news." This was a joke they shared. Their mothers talked on the phone at least every other day, even though they lived around the corner from each other.

"Let's hurry and get in our P.J.s," Jonas said. " 'Catch a Killer' is on in a few minutes."

"I don't really want to watch TV," Frankie said. "Can't I just stay in here and look at comics?"

Jonas thought it over. He was tempted. But he knew what his mother would say if he left Frankie all alone in the bedroom.

"Want to spy on Dan?" Jonas asked. "We could listen in when he calls his creepy girl friend."

Already in his pajamas, Jonas stared at Frankie. He was perched on the edge of the lower bunk like a zombie.

"Or we could work on my plane model and watch TV at the same time," Jonas suggested. He pointed to the model which was sitting on the dresser.

"Can't we just stay in your room?" Frankie asked again.

"Cripes, Frankie!" Jonas yelled. He stomped

into the bathroom and slammed the door. He squirted an extra-long worm of toothpaste onto his brush and began brushing furiously.

He stared at his face in the mirror but thought of his friend in the other room. He had gotten even gloomier since this afternoon, Jonas realized. What a poop, he said to his reflection. Okay, he's staying back. Does he have to ruin my fun, too?

A crash came from the bedroom. Jonas spit out the toothpaste, dropped his toothbrush on the sink, and yanked open the bathroom door.

"Oh, NO!" he cried. "DARN YOU, FRANKIE!"

Frankie's face was white. He was holding the left wing of Jonas's plane model in his hand. The rest of the plane lay at his feet, upside down.

"I'm sorry," Frankie whispered hoarsely. "I didn't mean . . ." He never finished his apology. Jonas raced across the room and threw himself on top of Frankie. Then they were on the floor, a squirming tangle of arms and legs.

Anger turned Jonas's face purple. "You broke

. . . it . . . on purpose!" he gasped. He had Frankie's arms pinned with his knees. Sitting on Frankie's chest, his own chest was pumping like a bellows.

"I did not!" Frankie shouted into Jonas's face. "I just picked it up and the wing came off in my hands."

"JONAS! Stop it right now!" Jonas's mother was standing in the doorway. "Get up immediately, both of you."

"He broke my model," Jonas said, sitting on the edge of the bunk. His hands were shaking and his breathing was loud.

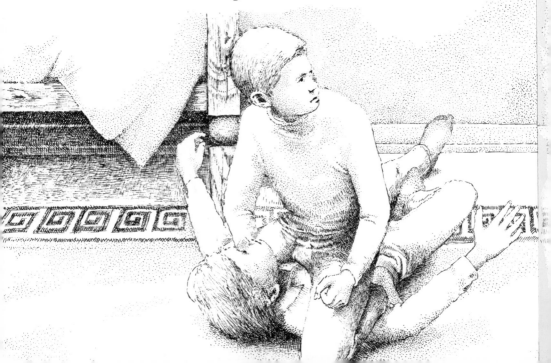

"I didn't break it on purpose," Frankie said, still sitting on the floor. His shirt was ripped at the neck. He had toothpaste on his cheek where it had met Jonas's chin.

The model had gotten kicked against a radiator. Other than looking lopsided, it hadn't suffered from the crash. Jonas's mother picked it up and placed it gently on the dresser.

She looked at the boys and shook her head. The tiniest grin was on her lips. "I thought a real plane had crashed," she said. "When you two are friends again, there's a snack for you in the kitchen."

Then she was gone. The door closed and the boys were alone.

Frankie fingered the rip in his shirt. He wouldn't look at Jonas.

Jonas picked at the drying toothpaste on his chin. He wouldn't look at Frankie.

Frankie scratched his arm.

Jonas scratched his head.

Frankie stretched.

Jonas yawned.

26

When there was nothing left to do, the boys looked at each other.

"I'm sorry," Frankie murmured. "I'll help you fix the plane."

"I'm sorry too," Jonas said. "I didn't mean to rip your shirt." He looked around the room. "Where's the wing?"

Frankie laid down on the floor and looked under the bunks. "I don't know," he said. "I was holding it in my hand when you jumped on me."

Jonas pulled the bunks away from the wall. The missing wing, wedged between the lower bunk and the wall, dropped to the floor.

"Here it is," Jonas cried. "Get my glue off the desk while I get some newspapers." He left the room and came back with a section of newspaper and a plate of cookies.

A half hour later the plane looked as it if had never been wingless. And the cookies were gone.

Jonas's father came in to tell the boys it was time for bed. "You guys did a great job on the model," he said, eyeing the plane where it sat on the bed. "How about hanging it from the ceiling so it doesn't have another accident?"

The boys laughed. "I've got some fishing line," Jonas said. Frankie went into the bathroom to put on his pajamas. When he came out the plane was swinging gracefully from the ceiling light.

"Look, Frankie, it moves." Jonas stood on tip-toe under the plane and blew. The breeze caught the wings and the plane turned in a gentle arc.

Frankie grinned. He folded his clothes, laid them on the floor, and crawled into bed.

Jonas's father poked them each in the ribs, gave the plane a spin, and flipped off the light.

"See you tigers in the morning," he said, and closed the door behind him.

"Night, Franko," Jonas said.

"Night, Jonas," Frankie answered from below.

"Jonas? If I stay back next year, will we still be best friends?"

"Sure," Jonas said, staring up at the ceiling. "Why not?"

Frankie took a long time to answer. "I don't know," he said finally. "Just all of a sudden I feel . . . lonely."

chapter 5

Frankie stared up at the model plane. The light from the window made it look as if it were flying in the moonlight. The plane looked real. It was real. It was coming in for a landing.

Frankie waited for the plane to touch down, holding his breath. His father was on board. In a minute the plane would taxi to a stop. The hatch would slide open. A pretty stewardess would smile as each passenger stepped into the night.

Frankie's father would be the last person to

leave the plane. Frankie would tear across the runway. His father would see him coming, and smile. He would run down the steps, his arms wide to give his kid a bear hug.

"Frankie? Are you awake?" The voice was Jonas's. Frankie blinked and rubbed his eyes. He'd been half-dreaming, half-pretending. In school Miss Minty always snapped him out of his daydreams before his father had a chance to get to him. Some day, Frankie knew, his father *would* get to him. He had to.

A shape hung over the edge of the upper bunk, blocking Frankie's view of the model plane. It was Jonas. "I got a new riddle book," he said. "You want to hear some?"

Frankie nodded in the dark. "Sure," he said. "Fire away."

Jonas clicked on the light over his pillow. Frankie watched his feet grope around, then find the ladder and climb down. Seconds later, the riddle book clamped in his teeth, Jonas climbed back into his bunk.

"Ready?" Frankie heard pages flipping. "Okay.

30

'How does the grocery-store owner stop people from stealing the bagels?' "

Frankie stared at the bulge in the mattress over his head. "I give up," he said. "How does he?"

"He puts LOX on them!" Jonas waited for Frankie's laugh. No sound came from down below, so he stuck his head over the side of the bunk.

"Get it? Lox and bagels?"

"Yeah, now I get it," Frankie said. "Lox and bagels, that's pretty good."

Jonas dropped the book onto Frankie's chest.

"Now you read me one," he said.

Frankie picked up the book. He held it away from his bunk to catch the light. On the cover, two kids were rolling on the floor, holding their sides. Tears ran down their faces. They were splitting with laughter.

"I don't really feel like reading riddles," Frankie said to Jonas's upside-down face.

"No fair," Jonas complained. "Come on, Frankfurter. I read you one."

Frankie opened the book to the first riddle. He

saw a picture of a bird with a tiger's head. He cleared his throat. Then he licked his lips. He could feel his heartbeats picking up speed. His eyes blurred and the words on the page ran together as if they were under water.

It was just like being in reading group.

"Well? Are you going to read it or not?" This time it wasn't Miss Minty getting tired of waiting. It was Jonas.

Frankie began.

"What-do-you . . . get-wha-when you . . ." He stopped. In school his face would be red. And burning hot. He was blushing now as he stared at the frustrating words.

Jonas lay silent in his bunk. He thought of the times he'd heard Frankie stumble like this in his reading group. After a long time he leaned over.

"Frankie? Can I help?"

Frankie didn't answer right away. "No," he muttered finally. "I don't like riddles anyway."

"No, I mean could I help you in school? Maybe we could do our homework together and stuff."

"It's too late," Frankie mumbled from below.

"Everyone wants me to stay back so I'll stay back."

"But that's dumb, Franko. Maybe if you . . ."

"WHO'S DUMB?" Frankie yelled. "Just because you and Heather Harrington and those other smarties think you're so great, don't go around calling other people dumb!"

Jonas heard a crash. He looked down. The riddle book was on the floor on the other side of the room.

Jonas was mad. To hell with him, he thought. Let Frankie stay back if he's going to act so jerky. Jonas switched off his light and rolled over.

Minutes later, as he was slipping into sleep, Jonas heard Frankie crying. He leaned up on one elbow, wanting to say something. What could he say? And hadn't he tried to help already and been yelled at? He flopped down on his back and stared at nothing.

Four feet from his head the plane spun lazy circles in the dark.

chapter 6

When Jonas opened his eyes in the morning, the first thing he saw was his model plane. Snuggled in his covers, he pretended to be the pilot. "Pilot to crew," he muttered, "prepare to abandon ship. Ready parachutes—JUMP!"

Jonas flung back the covers, perched briefly on the edge of his bunk, and jumped. The sound of his landing on the floor woke Frankie. He shot out of a deep sleep, eyes wide.

In three minutes Jonas was dressed and out the

bedroom door. In the kitchen, his mother was standing at the sink, dropping egg shells down the garbage disposal. The table was set for breakfast. Jonas counted the places.

"Who's not eating?" he asked his mother's back.

"Dan," his mother said, turning around. "He slept at Larry's house. Did you wash your hands?"

Jonas looked at his hands, then held them up for inspection. "See? Clean."

"Please wash them now," his mother said.

Jonas ran the water in the sink. "What's for breakfast?" he asked.

"It's not polite to ask the chef what's on the menu," his father said, entering the kitchen. He looked at Jonas. "I'm sorry about your arms," he added.

"What's wrong with my arms?" Jonas asked, checking them.

"Since your hair looks like squirrels combed it for you," his father said, pouring a glass of juice, "I assumed you'd hurt your arms."

36

"Aw, Dad, it's okay," Jonas said.

"Please go comb it, son."

Jonas returned to his room and found Frankie making his bed. He looked at his own tangled sheets and blanket and gave them a quick tuck and a yank.

Jonas sneaked a look at Frankie, wondering if he was still mad from last night. "Breakfast is almost ready."

"I'm not hungry," Frankie said, smacking his pillow into place.

"Mom's expecting you." Jonas headed for the bathroom. "You could be polite, you know."

He wet his hair thoroughly, attacked it with his comb, and ran back to the kitchen before it sprang up all over his head again.

Beth and his parents were sitting at the table. His mother was sliding waffles onto the plates.

"Where's Frankie?" she asked.

"Making his bed." Jonas popped a crumb into his mouth. He thought of his own bed and how it would look compared to Frankie's neat job. Then he remembered how Frankie had yelled at him and thrown his new book against the wall.

"You know that riddle book, that real simple one?" Jonas asked his father. "Frankie can hardly read it!" He gave a demonstration which made Beth burst into giggles.

"Beth, that's enough," Jonas's mother said. Then she looked at Jonas. Hard. "This is not the place to discuss Frankie's reading," she said softly. She got up to get some orange juice for Frankie, as he walked into the kitchen.

"I've cooked your favorite, Frankie," Jonas's mother said. "Waffles with honey."

Frankie sat in the empty chair between Beth

and her father. He stared down at his plate and waited for the conversation to pick up again.

But suddenly no one could think of anything to say. Jonas's dad stirred his coffee. His wife cut her waffle into tiny pieces. Jonas stuffed his, almost whole, into his mouth.

"Well, it's Saturday," Jonas's dad said, breaking the silence. "What are you boys doing today?"

Jonas glanced across the table at Frankie.

"I'm playing softball with some of the guys," he said.

Frankie acted as if he hadn't heard the question or the answer. He was very slowly cutting his waffle into bite-size pieces.

"How about you, Frankie?" Jonas's father continued. "Going to dazzle these chumps with your fast ball today?"

Everyone waited while Frankie chewed, then swallowed.

"I guess I'll just hang around at home," he answered.

Jonas's dad took a long sip of coffee. Eyebrows raised, he stole a look at his wife.

Beth put a sticky hand on Frankie's arm.

"How come you can't read Jonas's riddle book?" she asked.

Everybody froze. Mouths half-opened, forks in mid-air. It looked like a photograph of a family eating breakfast. But only for a split second. Then the table exploded.

Jonas smacked Beth on the shoulder. Her milk glass flew out of her hand and landed in the middle of the waffle platter. She screamed and knocked over her chair as she ran to her mother.

Jonas's father leaped to his feet. "That will cost you the rest of the weekend in your room!" he shouted to Jonas.

Cradling Beth with one arm, Jonas's mother mopped at the spilt milk with the other. She looked up to say something to Frankie, but he was gone. In his plate, his waffle lay sopping up honey.

Jonas sat rock still as he watched Frankie slip out of the room. He felt a lot of things, all bad. Guilt for hitting his little sister. Anger at his father's severe punishment. And shame for having told his family about Frankie and the riddle book.

He looked down at his sticky waffle and couldn't eat another bite.

chapter 7

The kitchen was quiet except for Beth's sobbing. Jonas and his father finished mopping up the mess the milk had made. The three remaining waffles had to be thrown away.

"Hush, now, Bethy," her mother said gently. "Jonas is sorry he hit you." She gave Jonas a look over Beth's shoulder.

"I'm sorry, Beth," Jonas mumbled.

Beth's breaths came easier, and finally the sobs ended. Her mother wiped her face with her napkin. "D-did I do so-something bad?" she sniffed.

Jonas's mother glanced up at her husband for help. He shrugged his shoulders. "Honey, Frankie doesn't feel well today," she said to Beth. "Why don't you go see if you can find him and tell him you're sorry he feels bad."

When Beth had gone her mother poured herself another cup of coffee. The cup rattled against the saucer when she lifted it for a sip.

"I feel helpless," she said. "I've known that boy all his life. If only his father hadn't left, maybe . . ."

"Honey, not now," her husband said, jerking his head at Jonas.

Jonas knew his mother was about to say something about Frankie's dad. He continued wiping the table, only slower.

"That's fine, Jonas," his mother said. "Now I think you need to find Beth and Frankie. I think they'd both like to talk to you."

Jonas shot a look at his mother, but her hair hid her face as she sipped her coffee. He threw the damp paper towels into the trash and left the room.

What am I supposed to say to Frankie? he asked himself. Is it my fault Beth opened her big mouth?

Everything had gone wrong since Frankie found out he was staying back. Jonas wondered when things would start to go right again.

He headed for his room to see if Frankie was packing up his stuff. The room was empty. No Frankie, no pajamas. Jonas ran out the front door and looked up and down the street. He saw a cat, but no Frankie.

Maybe he's in the fort, Jonas thought. He ran out behind the garage. His father had given him and Frankie permission to build a platform with sides in an old tree. It wasn't much, but they played astronauts up there away from the prying eyes of a certain little sister.

Jonas climbed up the ladder and peered over the top of the platform. He saw a pile of soggy comics. An apple core. A few bird droppings. But no Frankie. He pulled himself onto the platform and kicked the apple core. Then he sat down and leaned up against the tree trunk.

Some weekend, he muttered to himself. His best friend was mad at him. His family was mad at him. And for what? Nothing. All he'd done was try to help Frankie. Was he supposed to keep Frankie's staying back a big secret from his family? If he'd done that, Jonas knew, his family would have gotten mad at him for not telling them.

I can't win, Jonas said to himself. Why wasn't anyone mad at Frankie? He was the one who was staying back. Nobody ever got mad at Frankie, that's why.

A fat freckled face popped up over the edge of the platform. It was Blake Snyder.

"You gonna play softball or sit in your tree all day?" Blake asked. "All the guys are waiting!"

"I was just looking for something," Jonas said, scrambling to his knees. "Meet me out front. I've got to get my glove."

"Where's Frankie?" Blake asked, looking around. "We need him to pitch."

"No, we don't," Jonas said, jumping the last few feet to the ground. "I'll pitch today."

chapter 8

So where is Frankie, anyway?" Blake asked. They were cutting through Mrs. MacDougal's lot on the way to the park. "I never seen you guys not together on a Saturday."

"We probably won't hang around that much next year," Jonas said. "Frankie is staying back."

"Staying back? You've got to be kidding. Boy, wait'll the guys hear this!"

"You don't have to go blabbing it all over town, you know," Jonas said. He was already regretting that he'd told Blake.

48

"Why not?" Blake asked. "Everyone's going to find out anyway, aren't they?"

Yeah, Jonas thought, why not? Why should I worry about Frankie when Frankie isn't even thinking about me? All he's done is ruin everything and get me in trouble. And break my plane.

Jonas followed Blake as he led them over the short-cut route they'd been using since first grade. Behind Lolly's Rings 'n Things Jewelry Shop, across Jefferson Street, and through the parking lot in back of the Marco Polo Restaurant where Frankie's mom worked.

Jonas turned and looked behind him, down Jefferson Street. He hoped he wouldn't see the old station wagon Frankie's mother drove. He knew she worked at the restaurant on Saturdays, and it was just about time for the crowd that ate breakfast there before going off to play tennis and golf.

Jonas didn't see the car. He bumped into it.

"Jonas! Are you all right?" It was Frankie's mom. She was sitting in the station wagon combing her hair. Jonas had walked right into the fender. "I saw you looking over your shoulder, but I thought you'd seen me already." She swung out of the car and locked the door behind her.

"Hi, Mrs. Giordano." Jonas felt his face turn red. He picked at a crack in the parking lot with one foot and stared at it. He wished the crack would open up and swallow him. What if she asked where Frankie was?

"Isn't Frankie with you?" Mrs. Giordano did ask, looking around. Blake stood a few yards off, tossing a softball into the air.

The heat in Jonas's face spread to his neck. "He . . . um . . . he didn't . . . after breakfast he went . . . um, home, I guess." Jonas stared at the crack, and he knew Frankie's mom was staring at the top of his head. Her eyes were burning holes in the top of his baseball cap.

"He came home after breakfast?" she said. "That's funny, I drove by your house and I didn't pass him."

Jonas felt as if he was melting in the warmth of Mrs. Giordano's stare.

"Jonas?" She put her hand lightly on his shoulder. He half-expected it to burn, but it didn't. "Is everything all right? I mean between you and Frankie?"

Jonas squinted up, one eye shut against the sun. The lady looking back at him didn't have fire coming out of her eyes. It was just Frankie's mom, and the only thing coming out of her eyes was concern.

"You coming, Jonas?" It was Blake, tired of playing one-man ball.

"Run along and play, Jonas," Mrs. Giordano said. "I'm sure Frankie must have stopped off to do something. Keep an eye out for him, won't you? And tell your mom thanks for having him over last night."

Jonas watched Frankie's mother hurry through the back door of the restaurant in her white shoes and uniform. He and Frankie had teased her, calling her "Nurse Giordano" when she'd first shown them what she had to wear to work. Once she'd come out of the bathroom with a bottle of castor oil and chased them around the living room.

He was glad he hadn't had to lie when she asked about him and Frankie. But he hadn't said anything about what had happened at breakfast. Wasn't that like a lie? And where was Frankie anyway? If he hadn't gone home, where had he gone?

Nine kids were waiting in the park when Jonas and Blake got there, out of breath. Blake had insisted they run the rest of the way, seeing as Jonas had wasted so much time.

"What'd you do, forget your way?"

"Where you been, you guys? It's almost bedtime!"

The teasing came fast and heavy while they all scrambled to their feet and grabbed caps, gloves, bats, and balls.

"It isn't my fault, you guys," Blake put in. "Jonas had to stop and have this big conversation with a nurse."

"Where's Frankie?" someone asked.

"Yeah, where's our star pitcher?"

They were looking at Jonas. He was counting the fingers on his glove. "He couldn't make it," he muttered finally. Why did even thinking about Frankie make him feel so lousy? he wondered.

"That isn't all he couldn't make," Blake sounded off. "Wait'll you hear this." Blake had that look in his eyes that all kids have when they're about to let loose with some juicy secret. "Old Frankie's staying back!"

"That right? Hey Jonas, is he really staying back? Boy, I knew he was kinda dumb in school, but staying back? Wowee!"

"He's not dumb, and if you don't shut your stupid mouths you'll be sorry!" Jonas screamed. His breath was coming deep and short. Tears were crouched on his lower eyelids, waiting to slide down his face and embarrass him.

"Can we just get started?" Randy asked. "If I wanted to get into an argument, I could have stayed home."

The laughter that followed broke the tension and captains were chosen. Jonas volunteered to sit out the first inning since eleven players couldn't be split up evenly.

He found a tree to lean against, sat on his glove

and watched the first pitch. High and outside. The next was a little low, but Tommy caught the edge of the ball and sent it spinning past the first baseman.

If I'd been there I'd have snagged it, Jonas thought glumly. And if Frankie were here I'd be playing instead of watching.

Under another tree, fifty yards away where no one could see him, Frankie sat watching the game, too. He could see Jonas sitting out the inning, but he couldn't see Jonas's face. And he didn't hear Jonas stick up for him when one of the guys called him dumb.

After a long while Frankie stood up and walked slowly home.

chapter 9

Watching the pitcher, Jonas thought of Frankie. He knew they'd always be friends. He'd give him the weekend to cool down from being mad then, on Monday, everything would be all right again.

Jonas thought about all the fun he and Frankie had had ever since kindergarten. They'd always been on the same teams during gym and recess, worked on projects together in science. It had always been that way. And always would.

A cloud blocked the sun and Jonas wrapped

his arms around his knees. A sudden thought made him shiver: Frankie and he wouldn't have the same gyms anymore. They wouldn't even be together at recess. They would be in different classes with different teachers.

Nothing would be the same with him and Frankie anymore. How could it be? And what if Frankie made a new best friend? One of those creepy little kids in his class. No. Not Frankie. Not with a third-grader.

It was at that second that Jonas thought of the plan. It was such a simple, perfect plan. Why hadn't he thought of it before?

Jonas knew his mother couldn't make the school pass Frankie. That had been a dream. And Frankie had refused when Jonas himself had offered to tutor him after school. So Frankie would be a third-grader again next year.

The screaming on the ball field broke in on Jonas's daydreaming. The half-inning was over, sort of. As usual, the last out started a big argument because nobody on the team at bat could remember the other two outs.

Jonas picked up his glove and walked toward the yelling boys, still thinking about his plan. He'd put it to work on Monday.

Boy, was Frankie going to be surprised!

Jonas and his family went to visit his grandmother right after church on Sunday and got home late. Frankie didn't call and Jonas didn't call Frankie.

On Monday morning Jonas walked to school more slowly than usual, thinking Frankie might catch up with him. But he didn't. Frankie was already in his seat when Jonas walked into the room.

At 8:35 Miss Minty marched down the aisle, red pencil poised over her marking book. At each table she paused, glanced at the homework papers, then made an entry in her book.

Most of the pupils received checks alongside their names, but there were always a few who didn't have their homework. These received a zero for the day under the column marked Homework. Miss Minty never asked why the homework wasn't passed in. She just made a mark in her book.

Miss Minty stopped at Jonas's table. There were six kids but only five homework papers. The space in front of Jonas was empty.

Jonas looked up with an embarrassed look on his face. "I'm sorry, Miss Minty. I didn't get to do my homework this weekend."

A look of concern shot into Miss Minty's eyes. "Was someone in your family ill, Jonas?"

"No, I just didn't have time to do it." Jonas

looked down, opened a book, pretended to read. He felt the eyes of every kid in the room were on him.

The wall clock sounded like a bass drum to Jonas. Hours seemed to go by before Miss Minty moved. She made a clicking noise with her tongue, then gave Jonas his first zero that year.

Most of the kids opened their reading books now that the excitement was over. Not Heather Harrington. She leaned across her table and whispered to Patsy Carmichael, loud enough for the whole room to hear.

"The teacher's pet didn't do his homework. Bet she gives him a check anyway."

Heather glanced sideways to see if her remark had been heard by Jonas. It had. He made his famous monster-face at Heather: eyes rolled up, nose mashed, tongue hanging out.

"Pig!" hissed Heather.

"Was that you, Heather?" Miss Minty asked.

"No, ma'am," Heather lied. She blushed scarlet.

"Do you need extra work till I've finished?"

Heather went from red to white like a dying goldfish. She buried her face in her book.

On the other side of the room Jonas grinned.

"All right," Miss Minty announced, slapping her book shut and advancing to her desk. "You should all have read the next story in your reading books over the weekend." She shot a look at Jonas.

"Today in groups we'll read the stories together. Then I expect *everyone* to write out answers to the questions at the end of the story. In complete sentences."

Immediately there was a great shuffling of pencils, notebooks, and reading books. Usually everyone tried to do the questions before reading groups. That way they had free time to fool around while they should have been writing.

Miss Minty looked around the room, like an owl searching for a mouse. Actually she was trying to decide which group to call on first. Her eyes rested on Frankie's table, but she sighed and glanced away.

"Could we be first today, Miss Minty?" It was

Jonas. Twenty-four heads snapped around. Someone was asking to be first! Heather Harrington kicked Patsy under the table.

Miss Minty smiled at Jonas. "Of course, Jonas," she said. "And thank you for asking. All right.

Boys and girls, up front please." If Jonas realized the other kids at the table wanted to kill him, he didn't show it.

When the group was settled, Miss Minty asked who knew the name of the story that came next in their reading books. Tommy's hand shot up. " 'Miles of Monsters,' " he said.

"That's right, Tommy. Did you have a chance to read all of it?"

"Yeah," Tommy replied. "It's about a kid who has a part-time job in a factory that makes monster costumes. It's real scary."

"Good, Tom. Now let's find out what happens in this monster factory." Miss Minty looked around the group. She saw Jonas's hand up. "Will you read first, Jonas?"

Jonas cleared his throat, made himself comfortable, and began.

"One—day—Bill—Buh—Bowler—ans—uh, ans . . ." Jonas stopped and started again. He stopped a second time. "I'm sorry, Miss Minty," he said, shaking his head back and forth. "I guess this story is just too hard for me!"

chapter 10

M iss Minty stared at Jonas. Twenty-four third-graders stared at Jonas. Heather Harrington's mouth looked like the entrance to a tunnel.

"Would you like to try again, Jonas?" Miss Minty closed her eyes and stroked the side of her head.

Jonas stammered and staggered over the passage again, but with no improvement. Giving up, he smiled at Miss Minty and shrugged his shoulders. "I guess I just can't do it," he said.

"We'll talk about it after school," Miss Minty said, still rubbing her temple. "Mark, will you read, please?"

"One day, Bill Bowler answered an ad he saw in his monster magazine. The ad said: WANTED, BOY TO WORK IN MONSTER FACTORY. Billy cut out the ad . . ."

Somehow the day passed. But not as Jonas thought it would. Frankie was still mad, that was for sure. He sat with some other kids during lunch, and at recess he went to the nurse. When the last bell had rung, Frankie flew out the door with the rest of the kids, leaving Jonas alone with Miss Minty.

Jonas felt sick. This day was even worse than Friday and Saturday and Sunday. Now Miss Minty was mad at him along with everybody else.

Jonas watched as she straightened her desk and erased the boards. Finally she turned and looked at him. She stood there, just looking, for at least a whole minute before she spoke. "Will you bring your reading book up, please?"

Jonas was scared. Now Miss Minty would find out about his plan even before it got off the ground. What would she say when Jonas admitted he'd been lying when he said he hadn't done his homework? That he'd only pretended to be struggling over that simple monster story? That *he,* the smartest kid in third grade, was planning to stay back with his friend Frankie?

"I'm waiting, Jonas," Miss Minty said, breaking into his thoughts. He picked up his book and walked to her desk.

"Will you read the first page of 'Miles of Monsters,' please?" She looked serious as she stared at Jonas from behind her large glasses.

Jonas wished he'd never thought of his great plan, but it was too late to stop now. He began reading, and in his confusion he forgot to stumble over the words. He felt his face change colors, one after the other, like a Fourth of July display.

He started again. This time he was so flustered that it was easy to read one word at a time, with big pauses between each word. The way Beth read. The way Frankie read.

Suddenly Miss Minty's hand shot out and slapped the page. Jonas jumped as if he'd heard a gunshot.

"Just what do you think you're doing?" Miss Minty demanded.

Jonas looked up, scared, angry, confused. Miss Minty didn't look as if she was enjoying herself either.

Jonas was cornered. He stood, grabbed his book, and started to leave. Miss Minty stopped him with a lightning-fast hand.

"You stay right here, Jonas Freeman. I'm not finished with you," she declared. "I want an explanation for your performance during reading group this morning. And," she added, tapping Jonas's book with her fingernail, "for this ridiculous display. Just what are you trying to do?"

Jonas was near tears. His plan had failed. He was on a sinking ship. But he was getting off, fast.

"I'm going home!" he cried. "You can keep Frankie back but you can't keep me here!" He swallowed the sob that was hurting his throat, flung open the door, and raced down the hall.

chapter 11

When Jonas entered his house, his mother was talking on the telephone. He slipped into his room to do some thinking.

Jonas realized his plan hadn't gotten off to a very good start. He'd meant to sneak up on this business of staying back. Not do his homework on one day, flunk a test on the next. Something like that. But like everything else in the last few days, it hadn't worked. Plus Miss Minty was really mad at him!

And what about Frankie? Jonas had never

known Frankie to stay mad at him so long. Maybe I should have told him about my plan to stay back before trying it out, Jonas said to himself. Yeah, that's it. Frankie must be mad because I didn't tell him first.

Jonas decided to call Frankie but his mother was still on the phone when he reached the hall. She sat there nodding, holding the receiver to her ear, not saying a word.

Jonas knew it couldn't be Frankie's mom. When those two got on the phone they both talked at once and you could hear them laughing all over the house. Jonas's mother wasn't laughing. She was looking at him in a very strange way.

He headed for the kitchen, but his mother stopped him as he went past. "Yes, he's here, Miss Minty. I'll talk to him right away. Thank you very much for your concern. Good-bye."

She placed the receiver gently in the cradle and looked up at Jonas again. "That was Miss Minty," she said.

Jonas gave his mother a crazy grin. "Yeah? What did she want?"

"Let's talk in your room." Jonas's mother stood up slowly as if she were tired. Jonas walked ahead of her and sat on the lower bunk. His mother closed the door and sat down next to him. "Would you like to tell me about your day?" she asked.

Jonas stared at the floor. The back of his neck felt hot and prickly. Sure, he thought. First I threw away my homework, then I pretended I couldn't read.

"No," he whispered. He tried to count the sailboats on his bedspread but he had to keep blinking and lost count. Finally he stopped counting and stopped blinking and let the tears roll down his face.

His mother waited, then started talking in a soft voice. "Miss Minty told me you didn't have your homework, yet I saw you do it myself. That part doesn't bother me, though." She put her hand under his chin and raised his head so she could look in his eyes.

"What does bother me, Jonas, is that she said you were making fun of Frankie during your

reading group. Can you explain that, please?"

MAKING FUN OF FRANKIE! Jonas was flabbergasted. He wasn't making fun of anyone, he was . . . So that's why Frankie didn't wait for him after school. Jonas felt like laughing and crying at the same time.

His mother was staring at him. "Jonas?"

He tried to figure out the best way to explain what he had tried to do in school that morning. "I wasn't making fun of Frankie," he said finally. "Mom, if Frankie stays back, next year will be awful. He's my best friend and we won't have the same room or anything. We won't even get to eat together!"

Jonas's mother sat perfectly still. And she didn't take her eyes off him. Jonas knew she'd wait all day, if she had to, for him to finish.

He went on in a hoarse voice. "I made this plan, that if I didn't do my homework anymore, and didn't do well in reading and . . ." Jonas stopped and took a deep breath. ". . . Miss Minty would keep me back in third grade, too."

There, he'd said it. Funny, hearing himself say

the words out loud, Jonas thought the plan sounded pretty dumb.

His mother pressed her hands flat on her knees, smoothing away the wrinkles in her skirt. She tucked some loose hair behind her ears.

"Did you talk this plan over with Frankie?" she asked.

"No, why?"

His mother stared at him. Her eyes jumped all over his face as if they were looking for something. Finally they rested on his eyes.

"Because I have a feeling that it's not really Frankie staying back that's bothering you." She stopped and took a deep breath.

"Tell me the truth, Jonas," she went on. "Are you thinking of how dull your class will be without Frankie, or of how lonely and unhappy Frankie will feel when he's left behind?"

Jonas felt confused. His mom was saying that he'd been thinking only of himself. Had he? Was that why he wanted Frankie in his class bad enough to stay back himself? Had he really thought about how Frankie would feel next year?

A little. But mostly he'd been thinking about Jonas Freeman. He turned to look at his mother. She was smiling.

"It's hard when something bad happens to your best friend," his mother said. "Hard for both people, Jonas."

"It makes me feel sad," Jonas said. And for the first time, he did feel sad. For Frankie.

"And how do you think Frankie would feel if it were you staying back instead of him?"

Jonas hesitated. He'd never thought about that.

"I guess . . . he'd probably feel pretty bad too."

"Of course he would. Frankie cares a lot about you, just as you do about him. If he knew you were trying to stay back on his account, he'd be terribly upset." She put her hand on Jonas's head and gave him a little shake.

"Frankie is going through a lot of misery right now. He shouldn't have to worry about his best friend too. He needs a friend he can count on."

She looked at Jonas. "Why don't you go see Frankie and tell him what you've told me."

"He's mad at me," Jonas said, remembering Frankie's brisk departure after school. "I bet he thinks I was making fun of him, too."

"Oh, I think Frankie will know the truth when he hears it," she said, standing. "And I've had a talk with Frankie's mom and the school. They've also been working on a plan to help Frankie."

"Yeah? What?"

Jonas's mother laughed. "Help me make your bed and I'll tell you about it."

chapter 12

Jonas stood on Frankie's front porch and pressed the doorbell. When no one came, he pressed it again, longer. Still nothing. He stood on tiptoe and tried to look through the window in the door. A curtain blocked the view.

Where could he be? Jonas wondered. Frankie's mother got home around five o'clock and Frankie was supposed to stay in the house until she got there. It was only about 4:30 now. Where was Frankie?

Jonas sat on the steps and dropped his chin into his hands. Maybe something had happened on the way home from school. Maybe Frankie had run away. Any kid might run away if his best friend made fun of him in front of the whole class.

Feeling a little sick, Jonas shuffled to the sidewalk and looked up and down the street. He saw a speck that seemed to be growing bigger. He waited until he was sure the speck was human before he began to hope it might be Frankie.

Then he was sure. Frankie had a funny kind of hop when he walked. He raised himself onto his toes every time he took a step, almost as if he were trying to fly. Jonas ran to meet Frankie, waving his arms.

"Boy, was I worried," Jonas said. "I rang your bell about a hundred times and when nobody answered I thought you got kidnapped or something."

Frankie's excuse for not being home was the bag of groceries he carried. But he didn't say a word to Jonas. He just kept walking toward his

76

house as if he didn't even see the boy loping along beside him.

"Want me to help you carry that?" Jonas asked.

"No."

"Want to play a game till your mom gets home?"

"No."

Jonas wanted to ask Frankie where he'd been on Saturday, but decided not to. Frankie was acting too grouchy.

On the porch, Frankie shifted the bag to his other hip while he dug for the key in his pocket. Inside, he set the bag on the kitchen counter and began taking out bottles and cans. Jonas could have been on another planet.

Jonas sat on a stool and stared at the back of Frankie's head. He watched as Frankie folded the bag and stuck it between the refrigerator and the wall. He kept on watching while Frankie found a place in the shelves for every can, bottle, and jar.

"I wasn't making fun of you today," Jonas said at last. Frankie had to believe him, he just had to. Jonas's stomach was acting the way it had during

last year's class play when he'd had to ask the
princess to marry him.

Frankie left the kitchen. Jonas followed.
"Didn't you hear me tell Minty I hadn't done my
homework?"

Frankie went into his bedroom and started
fooling around with his fish tank. Jonas sat on the
bed.

"When I started reading funny it was because I
wanted Miss Minty to think I was a bad reader."
Jonas paused. "I wanted her to make me stay
back."

Frankie's hand stopped halfway into the tank.
Jonas knew he was listening.

"I made this plan that I would stay back too,"
Jonas continued. "It wouldn't be any fun if I was
in the fourth grade because we wouldn't get to
see each other all day."

Frankie turned around, his wet hand dripping
onto the floor. "You *want* to stay back?" he asked.

"I guess it was a pretty dumb thing to do. Anyway, it didn't work."

For the first time in a long time Frankie smiled

a real Frankie-smile. "Boy," he said, shaking his head. "Boy."

"Miss Minty called Mom and we had this big talk. I thought Mom would be ripped, but she stayed calm."

"I'm glad it didn't work," Frankie said.

"What do you mean?"

"I'm going to be in third grade again, right? But if my best friend is in fourth grade, I won't feel like such a little kid."

Jonas grinned. "I have this idea," he said, picking up Frankie's frisbee.

"Another plan?" Frankie was teasing him.

"No, listen. We can do our homework together every day after school. There's still almost two months till we get out. I could help you."

"Then what?" Frankie said. "I'm still staying back."

"Mom talked to the principal. There's this new summer crash program you could take," Jonas said.

"What's a crash program?"

"Mom says they give you help in just the stuff

you really need," Jonas said. "You have to go five hours a day and Mom says there's a teacher for every kid."

Frankie stared at Jonas. "You mean I'd have to go to school all summer?"

"You'd be out by two o'clock. We could still do a lot of stuff after that."

Frankie watched his fish zoom around in the tank.

"So what about next year?" he asked.

"Mom told me if you work real hard and do good, they might pass you."

"Fourth grade?"

"Yeah. You take these tests at the end of the summer to see how much you learned."

Frankie sprinkled some Vita-Bet fish flakes into the tank, snapped the cap on the container and walked to the window. After a long time he came back and sat on his bed again, next to Jonas.

"Will you really help me?" he asked.

Jonas let out a breath he hadn't known he was holding. And he realized how long it had been since he and Frankie had really talked to each other.

He grinned. "Sure I will," he said, spinning the frisbee on one finger. "Aren't we best friends?"

Frankie grabbed the frisbee and bopped Jonas on the head with it.

"Best friends don't give their best friends snake sandwiches," he said.

Then they both fell back on the bed and laughed until their sides hurt.

It felt wonderful.

About the Author

RON ROY lives in Hartford, Connecticut in an old Victorian house near Mark Twain's house. He travels every summer and enjoys many outdoor sports, including snorkeling, skin diving, and white water rafting.

Formerly a school teacher, Mr. Roy now devotes all of his time to writing for children. His previous Clarion title, *Breakfast With My Father*, was named a "Notable Children's Trade Book in the Field of Social Studies, 1980" by the National Council for the Social Studies—Children's Book Council Joint Committee. *Three Ducks Went Wandering*, another Clarion title, was a Junior Literary Guild selection.